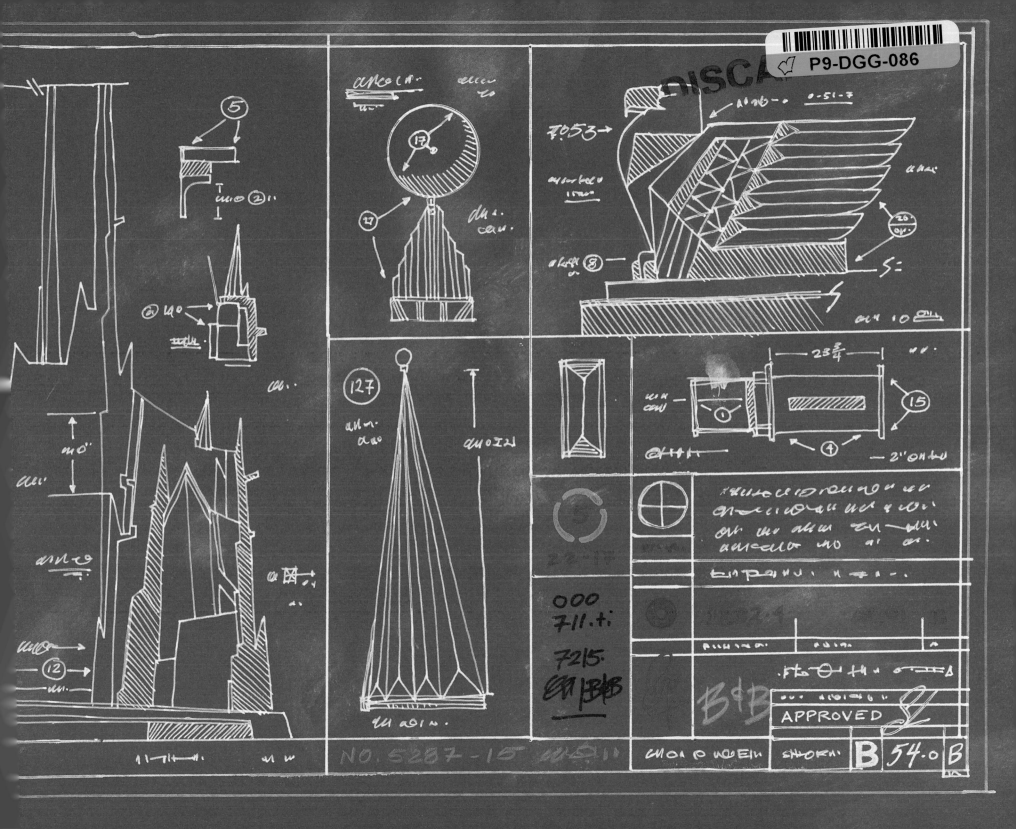

BUILDERS & BREAKERS

Library of Congress Catalog Card Number pending. ISBN 978-0-7636-9872-0. This book was typeset in Egyptienne. The illustrations were done in pen and ink and gouache.
Candlewick Press, 99 Dover Street, Somerville, Massachusetts 02144. visit us at www.candlewick.com.
Printed in Heshan, Guangdong, China. 18 19 20 21 22 23 LEO 10 9 8 7 6 5 4 3 2 1

To Richard Binder, the best engineer I know.
May you always break the rules and build wonders.

BUILDERS & BREAKERS

STEVE LIGHT

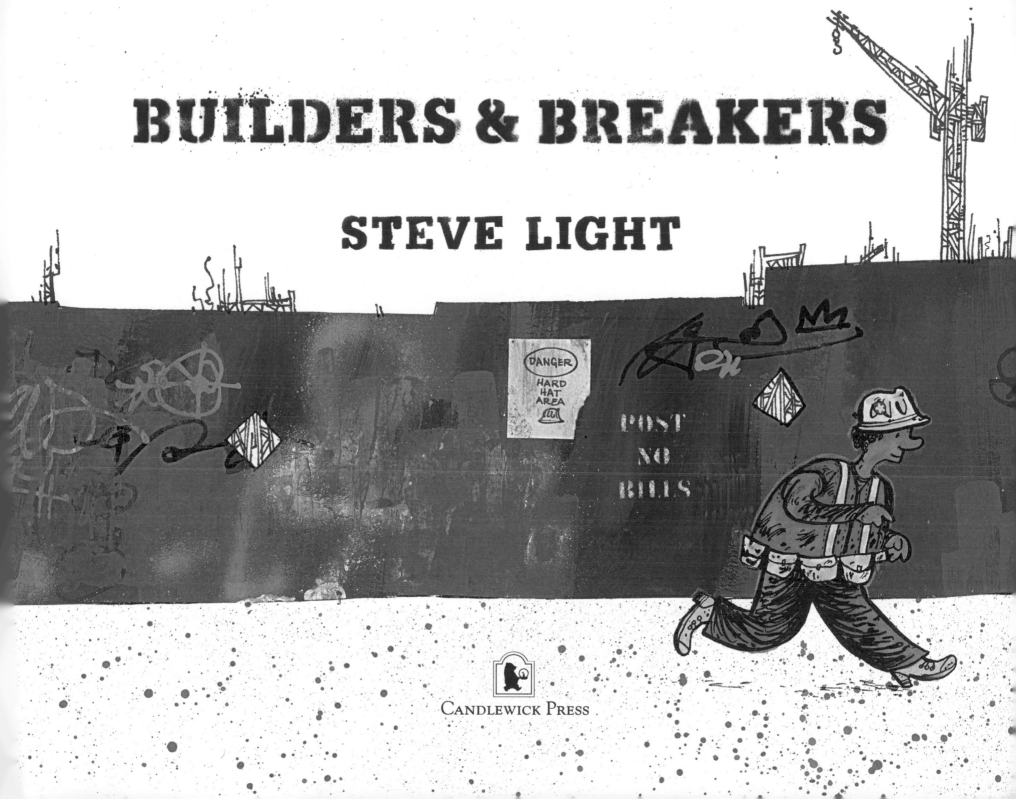

DANGER
HARD
HAT
AREA

POST
NO
BILLS

CANDLEWICK PRESS

Builders build.

Breakers break.

Building

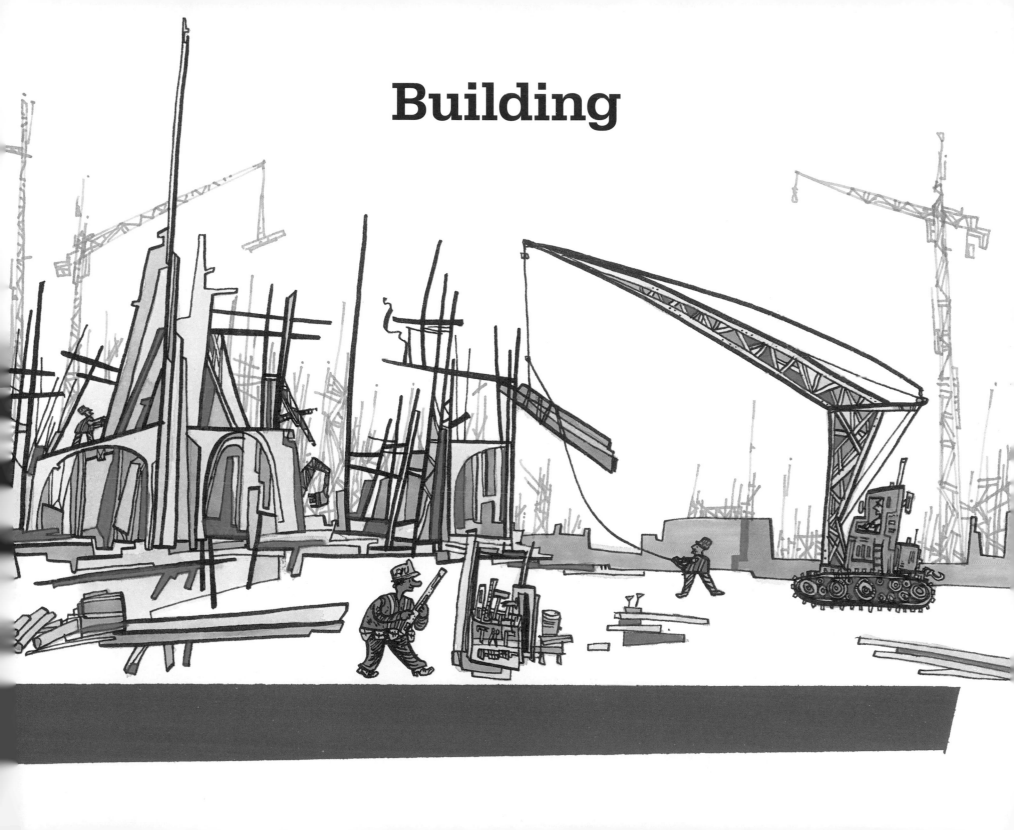

Break

Breaker

Breakthrough

Builders hammer

bang bang bang

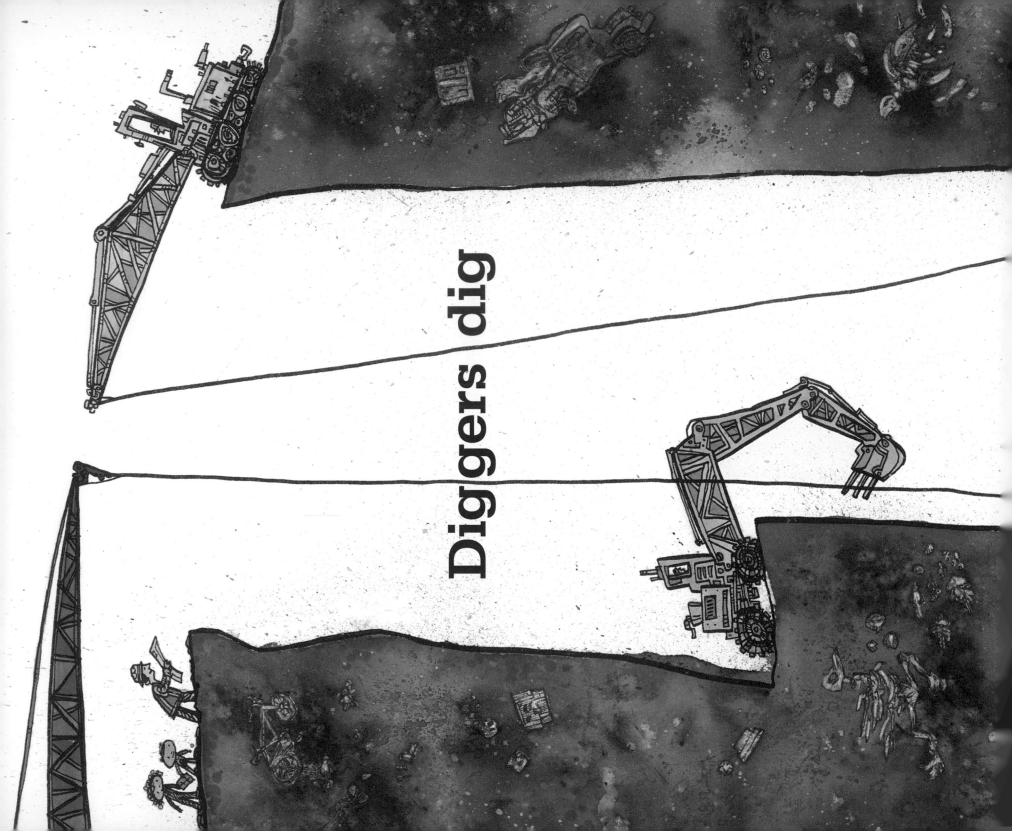

Diggers dig

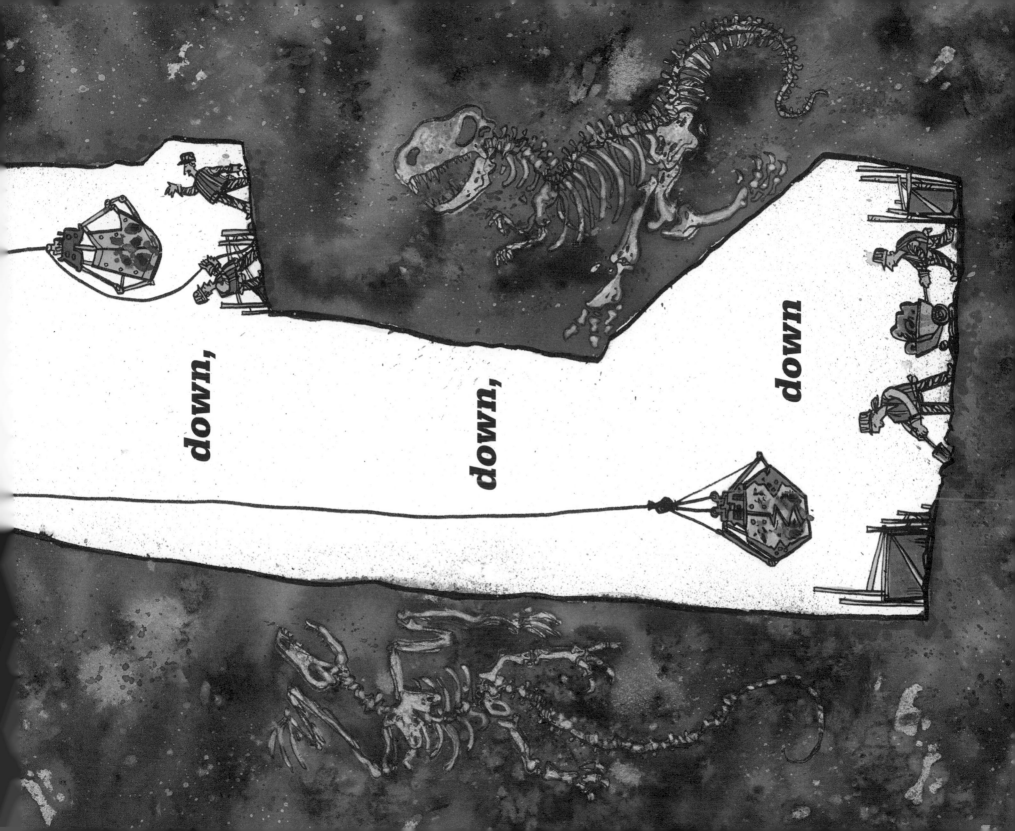

down,

down,

down

Welders weld

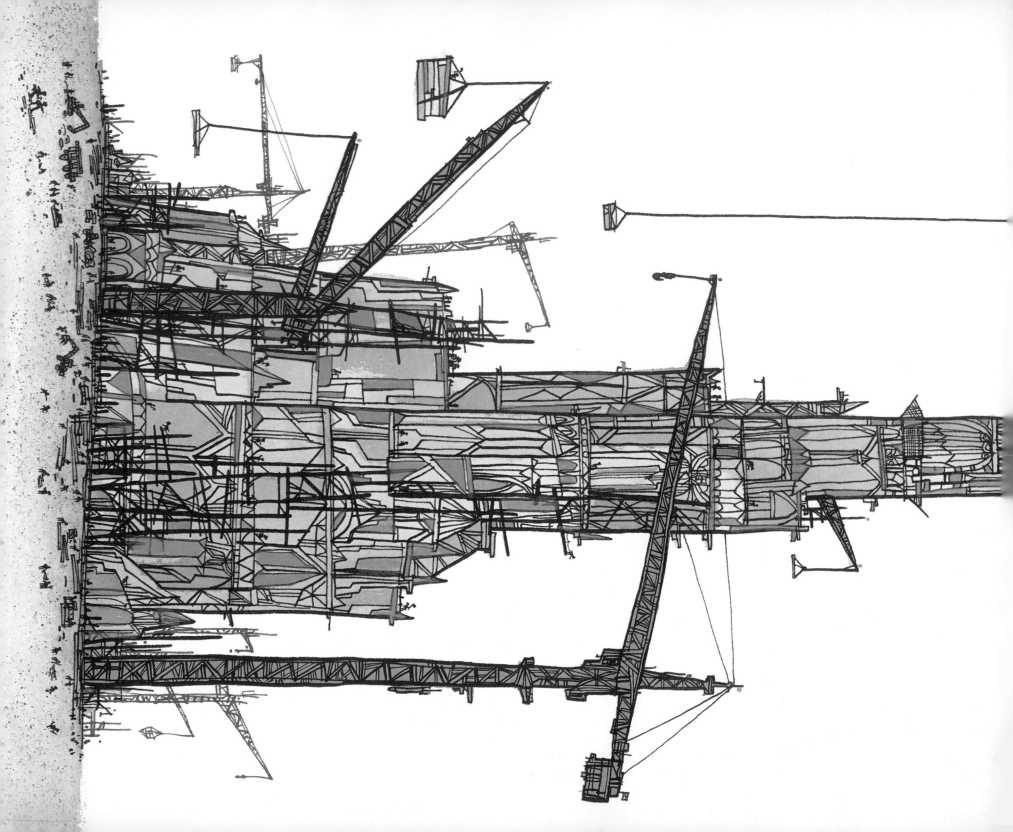

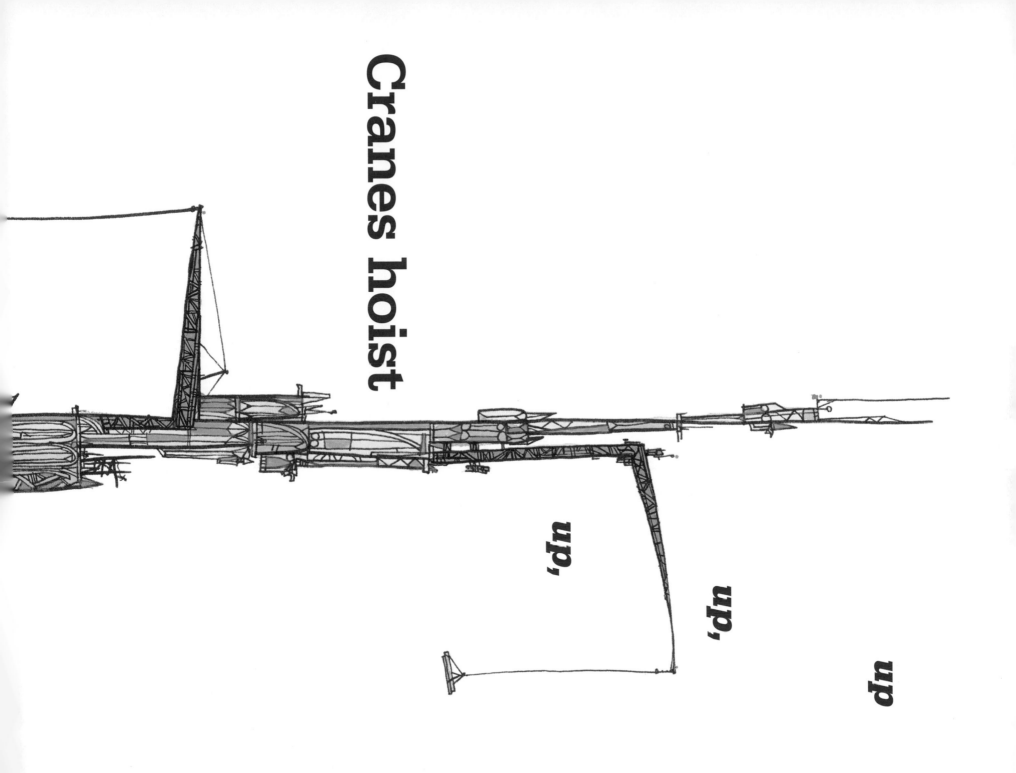

Cranes hoist

up, up, up, dn

Children search

look, look, look

Wheelbarrows carry

roll, roll, roll

After build time . . .

comes break time.

AUTHOR'S NOTE

Builders could not build without breakers to clear the way. Breakers could not clear the way without the builders' plan. It is a relationship that lets buildings be created and cities grow.

All the architecture in this book is drawn from my imagination. The designs of these buildings are pure flights of fancy. I did, however, find inspiration in classical, Gothic, and art deco architecture. I am fascinated by the domes in classical architecture, the flying buttresses of the Gothic period, and the beautiful geometric designs from art deco. All of these combined in my imagination. The results are buildings that I dream about.

To build anything, something else must be broken, even if it's just ground. It is this balance—destroying in order to create—that, we hope, leaves us with something of beauty.

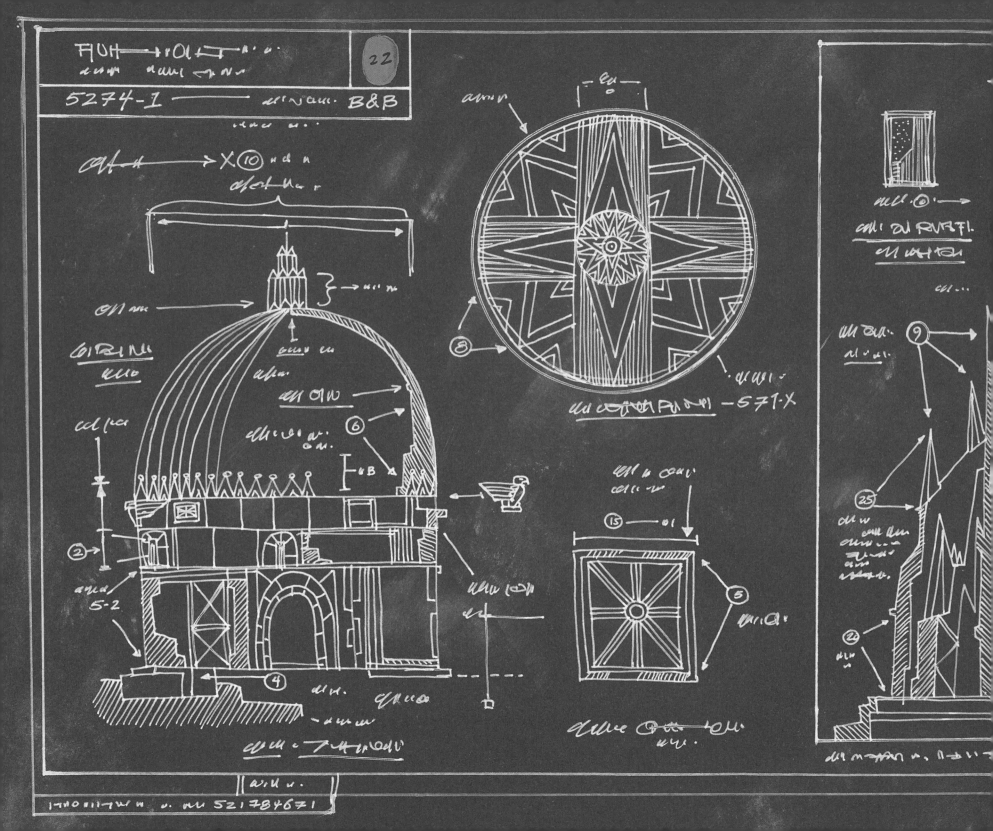